LIKE STILL WATER

A PREQUEL TO LOOKING FOR CLARA

SIMONA GROSSI

PIPES & CLOUDS

To Tomasella Scambia,
my piano teacher, my inspiration, and dearest friend,
who taught me most of what I know and love

1

"Clara? Clara...?"

Someone was calling my name but my mind was still on that beautiful Ravel's piano piece that I could not get out of my mind. It had the sound of water, perhaps the ocean, or a sea that I had never seen, but I seemed to know, from somewhere, sometime, from another life.

"Clara?"

Jeux d'eau. Water games. Ravel was immense.

"Clara did you like it?" My piano teacher asked. "One day you might study it."

I looked at my hands and thought they were too small to play it. That would never happen, I thought. The man who had just played it had huge hands and slender fingers, just the opposite of mine. Will they grow? One day? I was only 11 when I heard *Jeux d'eau*.

The end of the year recital at the Conservatory continued with other pianists, each playing different pieces, and yet my mind would not leave *Jeux d'eau* and Ravel. I couldn't wait to be home and hear that piece and other pieces by Ravel again and again. I knew Ravel, I thought I did. I had heard Ravel when I was four for the first time. It was the *Bolero*. Its music was so exhilarating, my heart could hardly contain it. It felt so big, too immense for me to grab it, own it. Years and years later, it still does feel the same.

I would close the windows to my bedroom, turn the light off, and dance to the notes of that piece. Ravel.

"Clara?"

It was Adam, my boss at the law firm. My memories must have played tricks on me. Adam had insisted that I go to a piano recital with him. The brother of a new client would be playing. "It'd be nice if we go. They expressly invited us."

I had not gone to recitals or concerts in years. Last time was before I quit piano, years and years ago. Adam begged me to go. "It's Ravel, I'm sure you'll like him. He was French." I had thought of telling him the truth, something like "You know, Adam, I was actually a pianist before law school. I know who Ravel is. I know, I've played his music," but I didn't. I remained silent, silenced my past once again, afraid of what that music might do to me years later, but I did go.

When the man started *Jeux d'eau*, a shower of memories paralyzed me.

"Clara? Did you like it?" Adam asked. That question sounded so much like my teacher's, when I first heard that piece. But there was no follow up, and I knew I would not get to play it. Not again.

I looked at my left pinky, the one I broke when playing volleyball with my colleagues during one of those stupid law firm retreats. I never took proper care of it and now it looked...not straight, wrong. Oh well, I knew I'd not use it again.

"You look sad. What's wrong?"

How would I explain?

"I'm just so tired."

"They're overworking you, aren't they?"

"You mean, *you* are overworking me?"

"Me? I'd honestly say you've been Elizabeth's property for months."

When the recital was over, Adam took me home. It was July, a gloomy, foggy L.A. night. I had left early that morning, when the sky would just make you guess what type of day that one would be: grey, sunny, chilly. You can never say from an early summer morning in L.A. You would have to wait until later during the day. I was still guessing, as I had been inside the office all day. Now the night was refreshing. I felt the ocean salt and breeze on my face, my hair, and yet the ocean was not that close. Was it *Jeux d'eau*? I smiled. I felt happier, not in the mood for bed, not in the mood for returning to my apartment. Had William been there, I'd have asked him to go out for drinks, a walk, a chat. But Adam was...different.

"Try to rest, Smith. You really look tired," Adam said when we arrived in front of my place. I thanked him, and headed to the door. I opened my window wide and smelled some intense flowers' fragrance. It hardly rained in L.A., but the previous months it had rained a lot. At times I had the feeling I was still in New Heaven.

I poured a glass of white wine, and pulled a Ravel LP to put it on the turntable and listen to it, face my memories, my past without anyone around wondering why I looked sad when I did. The wine would have helped. I had not touched that LP in years. When I pulled it from its cover, I noticed that the sun had damaged it. It was all curved. I had damaged it. I neglected it. My heart broke.

Please let it be OK. Let it play. I'd be better, I'd take better care. I withheld my breath as I put it on the turntable, moved the needle a bit, and waited. The needle struggled at first, but then it played, and it was…Ravel. A beautiful sequence of his work, immortal, so infinite, so ethereal. *Jeux d'eau, Pavane pour une infant défunte, Miroirs, Menuet antique, Gaspard de la nuit, Le tombeau de Couperin*…The notes were projecting photos of my memories, and they were all dancing, suspended in my room, as if hung on invisible laundry wires, hard for me to grab. At times I just wanted to enter them, but they were moving so fast, and they looked so far away, so distant from me, I could barely recognize me in there.

I had some of Ravel's sheet music with me. The piano, right there, close to the turntable, seemed to beg me to try one of them, but I did not. I couldn't even if I wanted to.

When the LP played *Ma Mère l'Oye*, I thought that collection of pieces came to calm me down. That was a perfect performance, and reproduction of my memories. I was 12 when I played it with a fellow student in my piano class. Four hands. How sweet, how great. I remember waiting for my partner in a naked, cold room, to finally enter the piano room where we would play. A fireplace, her mother bringing us cookies and tea, our chats about nothing, the rain, our dancing together to make what Ravel wanted. Were we ever close?

One of my boxes on the floor, still unpacked from when I moved from Connecticut, contained my books on Ravel, his life, work. I picked a few. Nobody actually knew Ravel, he was a mystery to many. Was he cold? Warm? Funny? Distant? Serious? What food did he like? What were his real, close friends? Did he take himself and his music seriously? Did he not?

As the record was still playing, I thought Ravel was perfectly clear to me, and I felt like him, with so much music inside that would clear any doubts about the person I actually was. Except, that music was trapped. Somewhere inside of me. A bottle on the ocean, that's what I was, with a cap someone or something had put on, long, long ago.

I moved to the desk, checked my Blackberry, and saw several new unread emails. None was about Ravel, my memories, and that music, so I thought they should wait.

Les entretiens de la Belle et de la Bête. Oh I remembered it so well. Everything now smelled again like those cookies covered in powdered sugar, everything seemed so easier back then, so natural. Where had all gone? Where was I gone? Tiers came from my eyes. I must be tired, I thought.

I pulled some paper from my printer, sat at the desk, and wrote.

Dear Ravel,

Or should I address you as "Maurice," as someone I know. I so wish we had met, I so wish we had been one in front of the other. I don't even know what I'd have asked you. I'd have probably just looked at you, remained silent, studied that mystery you were for so many people. Your music talks to me. It talks to me about you, and every time it tells a new story. Today I heard one of the pieces I used to play, one of yours. It was as hard as I had imagined. Listening to my piano pieces after so long was hard. I thought the pianist was great. I wonder if you'd have agreed. His technique was perfect, and I could hear the soul in his, your music. I could see, hear, taste the water of the fountains, watch the water play. And their light, strong, playful fire was shaking my still soul, calling it to wake up. Jeux d'eau.

What did you feel when you wrote Jeux d'eau? Was it truly that laughing river god tickled by the water that you imagined and wanted to write about? Your quotation on the manuscript did read "Dieu fluvial riant de l'eau qui le chatouille." Was it the sensuousness and grace of the fountains' game you were trying to capture? That effortless, impalpable grace, like in Régnier's poem? Or were you looking at the sea when you imagined Jeux d'eau? Was it a memory of the water that you contemplated once, a clear memory, one that did not leave you, that kept you company during one of your sleepless nights? One that kept you awake? Or was it just one of your mechanical objects, a mechanical, man-made waterspouts, where the water is channeled into repeated, uniform, almost hypnotizing patterns? Was it? This is what you somehow let people think. But was Jeux d'eau rather the product of your feeling suspended, gently moved by the waves of your life, by the events?

This is how I feel right now, although the music of my life doesn't sound so beautiful. Is there one? I still hear Satie and his Gymnopedies, their sadness. They come from far away, their sound not as clear as it used to be, but I know they're there.

Did I give up? A dream, an idea, me? My heart is like still water.

Dear Ravel, at times I wish I had lived your times, I wish we had met.

Clara

I finished my glass, poured another, and looked at my childish attempt to connect with my past. A letter to Ravel? I smiled. I wondered what someone would think of me if he or she found this. Should I just trash it? Instead I looked at it, carefully folded it, and put it in one of my suitcases. If I travel somewhere, someday, and I feel sad, I thought, I'll read it, or just look for Ravel's music, and I know this will make me feel better. And maybe somehow Ravel will find a way to reply to my letter.

2

"Clara? Clara?"

"Is it you? Wait? Really?"

He smiled.

"You are so short." I smiled.

"You're not that tall yourself, mademoiselle."

"This must be a dream. What year is this?"

"I agree with you. The pianist was good."

"Wasn't he?"

"You should try to play *Jeux d'eau* again."

"I can't. I haven't played it or played piano in…"

"Your hands will follow your mind, and heart. Just jump."

"Jump?"

"Where?"

He looked at me, his skinny persona with deep eyes.

"The water?"

3

The next day, when I woke up, I felt so happy. That dream felt real, and yet so beautiful and distant from my own reality. I needed a break. I needed, wanted to jump, but where? I had no idea. Was it the water? I could go to the ocean, spend the day on the beach, but there was so much work to do, deadlines, meetings. No, I could not call in sick.

I made coffee and looked for my Ravel sheet music. *Jeux d'eau* was there, with stains of coffee and tea, several ideas on the margin, in pencil and pen, a lot of drawn glasses (my teacher's way of signaling to me that I should pay closer attention to a passage) and metaphors here and there to remind me of the sound that I should try harder to create. Inside the sheet music there was a brochure for a master-class on Ravel I never attended. It was supposed to happen sometimes after my last concert in Brussels, but never did. I remember receiving a phone call from the organization. They wanted to know where had I disappeared. They explained they could not give me my money back if I had not shown up. At that time, I could not care less. The man who was offering the classes was Russian, Sergey Kissan. I looked for him on the internet. The name sounded familiar. How come I remembered it so well.

He lived in San Francisco, had married an American actress and would be performing in L.A., with the L.A. Philharmonic, in August. But no, that wasn't the reason I remembered his name well.

I took a shower and dressed. For no reason whatsoever, at least not one I could understand, I placed my *Jeux d'eau* sheet music in my briefcase and left.

Elizabeth was standing at the reception desk when I arrived.

"Good morning! You look different."

"Different? How?"

She shrugged her shoulders waiting for me to explain, but I had no idea.

"Did you remember we were supposed to meet that Russian client?"

"Russian?"

"Yes. Perfect, not even you remember. Nobody seems to remember. We don't even have a room reserved. This team is losing it. Miriam? Get us a room."

Miriam's computer was open to the meetings page, I checked and saw "M. Kissan, 10 a.m."

"Who's Kissan?" I asked Elizabeth.

"What do you mean? He's our client. His company might have patent and trademark claims against DIG. Your stuff."

" 'M.' Kissan?"

"I think he's Mikhail. Why? Do you know him?"

That's where I saw Kissan's name. He was the pianist we went to see with Adam the night before. And the teacher whose class I never took. Ravel was probably replying to my letter.

"No," I said, "but last night, Adam and I just saw his brother's recital, I guess."

"Oh, you guys went, I'm so glad. I was supposed to go but the Turig case exploded yesterday. I might need you on that too."

I went to my office, collected my file, browsed my agenda, then closed my eyes and thought about my dream.

"Jump."

I opened my eyes and looked outside the window. A collection of ugly, tall grey and brown buildings, with their big, dark windows hiding many little boxes like the one I was in, and a street filled with colors, trash, and chaos. Where would I jump?

I opened my briefcase, pulled my Ravel music, and for a moment I saw him again, like in a day dream, from which Miriam woke me up. "It's time," she said. "Everyone is in Room 5."

"I'll be there in a minute," I said, rose, and walked to the room.

There were five people in there: Elizabeth, Adam, and three men I did not recognize. The clients, I thought.

"Mr. Kissan, Mr. Sokolov, this is Clara Smith, our associate who'll work on your case."

I shook their hands and turned to their right. I didn't know the man in the forties sitting there, and looked at Elizabeth for clues.

"Frank Minst, Clara Smith. Frank is our associate from the Munich's office. He specializes in intellectual property. I thought you two could work together as he's here."

I smiled and shook his hand as well. Frank was blond, pale, a little taller than me, green eyes, rigorous look, but not terribly in shape. He seemed nice.

Mikhail Kissan had an extremely elegant figure: thin,

white hair, very deep and penetrating look, black eyebrows, perhaps his original hair color. His voice was soft, his hands barely moving as he talked. He looked anything but Russian. In fact, he could have been French. He did look like Ravel. Or my deep desire to make my dream real suggested that. Mr. Sokolov was skinny, tall, a little curved on himself, with a big curvy nose. He was also elegant, and seemed to be there to make sure that Kissan received the assistance he needed.

Sokolov described their claims. Their company produced and sold "fresh" juice whose distinctive features, among others, was its packaging.

"We had a designer come up with a new concept of bottles that are becoming famous in Russia and abroad. We think they played a big part in the success of our products. Now we have come to know that DIG is about to use very similar bottles and a very similar logo to sell its own yogurts and we want to stop it, and do it fast."

"That makes sense," said Elizabeth.

"Let's see the bottles and logos. How do we know DIG is actually doing this?" Adam asked.

"We have received confidential information from reliable sources," Sokolov replied, as he handed Adam and Elizabeth a brochure with the photos of the products and their logo.

"We'd need evidence of the breach," I said.

"You obviously have a patent and trademark for the bottles and the logos. We'll need the relevant documentation," added Frank.

"Of course," said Sokolov.

We discussed timing and place of the lawsuit. DIG's headquarters was in Delaware, but they wanted to sue in L.A.

"Why L.A.?" I asked.

"I must confess it'd be more convenient for us. My brother and I will be here for a while as he's working on a movie and he's not being well recently. So we want to take care of this here, as we are in L.A. "

"On a movie?" I asked.

"Yes, he writes music."

"Sergey?"

"Yes. How do you know him?"

Jump.

"I think I heard his name, read something. And Adam and I went to his recital yesterday."

Jump.

"Did you like it?"

Jump.

"I, yes, sure."

"If you like his music, he'll be playing with the L.A. Philharmonic on August 13. It'd be an honor to have you there."

Jump.

"Thank you. I'd very much like it."

"He'll be playing Ravel, Piano concerto in G major."

"Ravel?"

"Yes, he has a PhD in Ravel's work and his time."

"I know." Jumped.

"You do?"

"I must have read it."

4

Frank and I worked well together on Kissan's case. Indeed Kissan was right. DIG was about to infringe on Kissan's company patent and trademark, with Kissan's bottles being used not only in the U.S., but on all DIG's markets world-wide. Thus, what started as a local action in the U.S. turned into a series of actions also filed in Europe, Asia, and Latin America.

Frank and I flew to Paris, Singapore, and Brazil in less than 10 days. I knew we visited those cities only because I read their names on our dockets, my flight tickets, and at the airports once we arrived at each destination. Other than that, we moved between hotels and law firm offices, always in taxi, sometimes when it was too dark to distinguish people and buildings, other times when the light was so strong for our eyes to even see anything at all. Or my eyes were so sleepy and I was so jet-lagged that I barely noticed what was happening around us. Also, everyone we spoke to, spoke perfect English. Did we truly go anywhere outside the U.S.? I could not say.

We studied tons of documents, worked on memos,

briefs, talked to people, had two court appearances, meetings with experts. All of this in a little more than three weeks. When we were done, or at least the major part of it was, I collapsed. That night I was supposed to go to the concert, and despite how tired I was, I could not wait.

The Philharmonic was as beautiful as I had imagined it. Although I had been in L.A. for quite some time, I had never been there.

Jump.

The place was packed, and people were still arriving. Mikhail and I were seated in the very first row, from which I could clearly see the piano, placed just close to the edge of the stage. Each player was at his or her place, trying their instrument, this or that passage, smiling, moving the sheet music, the stand. Preparation time had always been exhilarating to me. The concert master led the tuning of the other instruments, there was silence, and then the conductor appeared. A young woman wearing simple but cute, black French pants, blouse, and flats. A little *Madeline* in adult clothes, with vibrant eyes, that would reach across the room and pierce it. I was enchanted.

Sergey Kissan followed her. The audience welcomed him with a warm applause. He must have become famous as I was busy studying law. He had not changed much from the picture in my old master class brochure. A little chubbier, still short and pale, with rebellious curly hair, and what seemed huge hands. My teacher at that time had insisted that I take his class. She thought he was fabulous. At that time there was no internet, so I only knew about him what she had told me. Now there he was. I smiled, happy to be there. I jumped, I thought, somehow.

When the music started I remembered it. So joyful, so beautiful, and when the piano made its entrance I could not contain the tears. I tried to hide them from Mikhail but I think I did not succeed. Sergey was perfect, light, precise, assertive, but joyful, crystal clear, enjoying the music immensely without letting the pleasure control his performance. The perfection Ravel was looking for. It was there, staged for us to savor. I heard it and saw it. Sensual and exotic phrases dancing around more nationalistic ones, the nineteenth century flirting with the twentieth one, people's and nature's stories, a love story, all in there. I was so happy. I seemed to hear all my favorite music in that piano concerto, as if that single piece contained Ravel, Gershwin, Satie, all together, in a story that was my story, one that only I knew. That loneliness made me happy and sad at the same time. I was happy that someone had captured my soul, could speak to me so well. But sad that he was no longer alive. I could not talk to him, share what I was feeling, myself.

Then Sergey Kissan played *Valses Nobles Et Sentimentales* in the solo piano version, and it was perfection as well. It really seemed as Ravel had come back to play his music years later.

When the music stopped I felt emptied, as if I had jumped into the water, the ocean or the sea, drank it, and cried it out. My entire soul had been washed. I could barely talk. My law-firm-me suggested a drink to calm me down but I wasn't sure I wanted that, as I didn't want to kill whatever I had turned into. I wanted to see it, even if people might see that too.

"Are you OK?" asked Mikhail.

"I'm fine. Just shaken."

"It was beautiful to see you react like that. I had never witnessed anything quite like it. Sergey is wonderful, but your reaction was...moving."

"I'm sorry. It has been so long."

He looked at me trying to understand what I had just said, but did not dare ask more.

"I should probably go."

"Would you like to meet Sergey?"

Jump.

"I don't think I could actually talk to him right now."

Jump.

"I'd better go," I added, and left.

5

A little over a week later, we learned that we had won the leading Kissan/DIG case. The other actions mirrored that one, so we were confident we'd win all the others. As I was writing an email to inform Mikhail, he called. He did not know about the case, but was calling me to invite me to dinner with his brother and his brother's wife.

"I told Sergey how moved you were from his music, and he said he'd love to meet you, if you have time. We're going to have some friends from the orchestra over for dinner Friday night. It would make us so happy if you and your team would join."

I said I would go. In fact, to my own surprise, I was looking forward to meeting Mikhail again. He so reminded me of Ravel and yet, how ironic, he was the opposite of a musician: a construction project manager, who probably attended his brother's concerts more out of courtesy towards him than out of interest and passion for his music.

I told Elizabeth about the invite. She said she would think about it.

"It has been quite an intense month for me," she said on

Friday afternoon. "I need a break from clients. You should go and have fun."

I had not considered going on my own but I could not cancel, and I didn't want to. It was only 5PM when Elizabeth left the office. I had more work to do, but I was tired. I tried to find the enthusiasm and focus somewhere between news webpages crowded with advertisements, but I did not succeed. I turned off the computer and left. I could walk to Mikhail and Sergey's place, it'd probably take over an hour, but I didn't mind. The mirror in the lady's room was not nice to me. I needed a shower and a fresh dress, but I didn't feel like putting any effort into this, and I could not even explain why, as in fact I wanted to go.

When I closed the door to the office behind me, the sky looked so surreal, cotton clouds hiding the sun, but it wasn't dark. The light was actually making my eyes tired, or I probably had not slept enough. I walked for a while, holding my briefcase. I was wearing my comfortable, anonymous Friday shoes, so I walked and walked, until I felt too tired to continue. The dinner wasn't until 8PM, but it was only 7PM. I thought I should try to recover some energy, get a coffee or something, so I looked for a coffee shop, but there seemed to be none, not one where I'd feel comfortable enough. After a while, I felt I needed a restroom. When I passed by a luxury hotel I had been to before, I could not resist.

I entered and headed to the lady's room. I thought I could stop at the bar inside the hotel right after, and relax there a bit before heading to the party, maybe by taxi. The lady's room was filled with mirrors and benches that were so inviting. Their design seemed to be antique, French, or at least I imagined they'd be. I noticed that my battery was running out but saw a place where I could charge my phone. I could stay there and wait for the phone to recharge, and then go to the bar. I plugged my phone in, took off my shoes, and put on the headphone with some Ravel music. I fell asleep, and I dreamt.

I was walking bare foot in the hotel, following the sound of a piano that was coming from somewhere inside the hotel. The hall was filled with people, but they did not seem to notice me. I wanted to ask them if they could hear the piano, if they could tell me where the sound was coming from, but when I opened my mouth, no sound would come out. No matter how hard I tried, I could not speak. And then I realized I was invisible too.

That should have frightened me, but it did not. I stopped trying, and I kept looking for the piano, until I found it. The room was magnificent: the walls were tall, ivory, with wide, classic paintings, and wide windows covered by silky, creamy curtains, and giant carpets on the floor. I pressed my bare feet on them, and felt happy, liberated, like a baby who was given permission to play. I turned my eyes up and saw majestic chandeliers pending from the ceiling, with a shower of crystals, some of which were reflecting a ray of sun that had made it through the heavy curtains. The room was almost dark, but in the distance, I saw the piano. There it was, an elegant, shiny, gloss, black grand piano, open without a player, its white keys shining.

I moved closer and opened the tail, and when I did, loud and playful water waves overwhelmed me. I squeezed my eyes, but nobody was playing. And yet I could hear *Jeux d'eau*. I sat on the bench and saw the sheet music. I turned to see if anyone was there, but I was the only one in the room. If I'm invisible and can't talk, I thought, maybe nobody will hear me play either. I should try.

I pushed my fingers against the keys and started playing. I did not remember much, but then I did, something, and I played. I felt so happy. At first my attempts were clumsy, but then something came out nice, and more, and more.

"Miss?"

"Just a moment, I have to try one more thing."

"Miss?"

A cleaning lady was gently moving me to see if I were fine.

"Oh no, what time is it?"

"Nine."

"What? PM?"

"Yes," she replied, and smiled.

I rushed out the door without shoes and had to return and collect them, to run again towards the lobby and then out, to call a taxi.

Fortunately, I wasn't that far from the Kissans' place, but I arrived there at half past nine. When I was introduced to the big living room where all the guests were, I was pleased to see that the dinner was a buffet. Nobody had been waiting for me.

"I'm sorry for being late," I told Mikhail, as soon as I saw him.

"It's OK. I understand, work is work," his voice was polite.

"It wasn't work. I just fell asleep on..." Would he ever believe me? "Never mind."

"Clara, this is Sergey," Mikhail turned to his right, and his opposite appeared. Sergey's cheeks were even chubbier than I had noticed when I saw him perform, and so red. And I was right about his hands. They were huge. His hand shake strong, almost hurting.

"Miss Smith, Mikhail told me he was impressed by your reaction to my interpretation of Ravel's piano concerto."

"Yes, you understand Ravel. I mean...in my opinion you do."

"A lawyer who understands classical music. That's unusual."

"Is it?" Mikhail asked.

I smiled.

"The truth is, I've studied Ravel and his music for so long, and yet it appears as a mystery to me."

"The man or his music?", I asked.

"Aren't the two deeply connected?"

"Definitely."

"Do you know Ravel?", he then asked.

"His music? Yes, I think I do."

"What's your favorite piece?"

"My favorite? There are so many. I have *Jeux d'Eau* sheet music still with me. I used to play it."

Jump.

"Really? You must have been serious with piano."

Jump.

"I enrolled in your master class about...ah...well, several years ago. But I did not show up."

"My master class? Where?"

"Somewhere in Connecticut."

"That must have been seven years ago or something?"

"Maybe. Too painful to remember."

"Painful?"

What did I do?

An older lady came to grab Sergey and I remained alone with Mikhail. He looked at me for a while, perhaps waiting for me to add to what I had just said, or simply change subject. But I was probably too tired to even decide for the first or the second option. So he decided for me.

"Are you hungry?"

"I'm...thirsty."

"Champagne?"

"A sweet one?"

"Sure," he said, offered his arm, and took me to the table where waiters and sommeliers were serving alcohol. He whispered something in one of the man's ear, then turned to me.

"Don't worry. Mine are good intentions. I just want to surprise you."

The man in black and white uniform pulled a bottle from beneath the table, opened it, and poured the champagne into two elegant flutes, then gave one to me and one to Mikhail.

"To the good memories."

"Yes," I said. "To the good memories."

"Come with me, I want to show you something," he added. I followed him and we walked out of the big living room, and wandered through long and semi-dark halls until we reached a darker room. When there, he turned on a lamp, and invited me to enter. Then he moved to a balcony, opened its tall doors, turned toward me, offered his hand, and said,

"You have to see this."

I walked toward him and my eyes were trapped in so much beauty, that also seemed familiar. I could smell jasmine. Maybe it was that fresh and intense fragrance that gave me that impression.

"I'd been looking for jasmine so hard when I was in Connecticut," I said, and smiled, happy.

"Well, hard to find it there. Isn't it?"

The sky was so filled with stars, and their light gently illuminated a delightful little garden, with a short stone path and what seemed stone steps on the left, all surrounded and partially hid by little precious plants of different species, all carefully shaped. They almost looked like giant and precious green flowers, although I could not see them clearly in the dark. If I closed my eyes, though, I somehow could. I could sense their fresh, intense green.

"What do you think?" he asked.

"It's beautiful."

"I thought you might like it, as you like Ravel."

"What do you mean?"

"Doesn't this remind you of something?"

I remained silent, trying to search my memories but couldn't find any sign of that garden in there. And yet, that garden did look familiar.

"I also like Ravel very much. I don't know him and his music as well as you and Sergey do, but I have read a lot about him, and I have seen photos, and watched documentaries of his beautiful house close to Paris. When I bought this house for Mikhail, I wanted to surprise him and recreate that garden that Ravel used to contemplate from his balcony."

"Oh, *La Bélvèdere*."

"Yes, his house. *La Bélvèdere*."

"Did you see it? Did you go there?", I asked.

"I was going to, but then I didn't. Painful memories, perhaps like yours?"

I looked at him. The night was really playing tricks on me. He looked like Ravel.

"I'm sorry. I didn't mean to intrude. And we toasted to good memories, didn't we?"

"We did," I smiled.

"Maybe our duty is to turn painful memories into good ones."

I thought about my memories. It'd be impossible to succeed in my case.

"Right..."

"You don't sound so convinced," he said.

"I'm not," I said, I looked around and remained silent for a while.

"What do you like so much about this garden?" I then asked.

"It gives me peace. It's beautiful, almost perfect. Perhaps it can be perfect because it's small. It's manageable. At times I feel we pursue things that are too big, too hard to handle. We want them to be perfect, but they'll never be. They are too far from our reach. This garden is...small. I can look at it all from here, my eyes can hug it entirely. I can check the growth of this or that plant, the flowers, the trees, and still get surprised when new flowers make their appearance, or when I notice little sprouts here and there...And our cats can go around without getting lost. It's a beautiful painting. Right there. That beauty and dynamic and unpredictable order keep surprising me, give me peace."

"You are an interesting engineer."

"Why?"

"I didn't imagine an engineer to be so..."

"So?"

"Artistic. Almost poetic..."

"I wish I could play the piano. If I played piano, I'd never stop."

I must have turned sad.

"I'm sorry. Did I say anything wrong?" he asked, and placed his hand on mine. I felt warm, and pulled my hand away.

"I think I should go. I'm getting so tired."

"Of course. Thank you for coming. It was nice seeing you again."

We walked in silence toward the door. He asked me if I had left anything in the wardrobe room that I should retrieve, but I impulsively said no. There were a few cars waiting in front of the entrance door. He nodded to one of the drivers, the black car approached, he opened the door for me, I entered, he bowed, kissed my hand, and closed the door for me.

I pushed my head against the window of the car and slept until I arrived home.

I took a warm bath and thought about what had happened that night. All seemed so unreal: falling asleep in that hotel luxurious lady's room, the party, the chattery, *La Bélvèdere*, and Mikhail almost looking like Ravel and suggesting that I should turn the painful memories into good ones. He spoke to me as if he knew me. At another time, I would have shared all of this with William. I checked my phone and last text from him was...from last Christmas. The usual "Merry Christmas. I know you won't reply to this, but I was thinking of you and hope you're celebrating and happy." A message for Christmas, one every year. The previous one was from the Christmas before, and before.

I pulled a towel from the hanger, and went to my bedroom looking for *Jeux d'Eau*, not sure why. It was past mid-night. I would have not played at that time. I couldn't. But I wanted to. As soon as I rose from the bathtub, I realized I had left my briefcase at Mikhail and Sergey's place. I didn't need my notes for the weekend, but *Jeux d'Eau*...

6

The next morning I woke up with a terrible headache. I didn't have much wine the night before, but it all still felt like an inebriating summer dream. The only evidence that it wasn't, was that I had indeed left my briefcase at that gorgeous house. The other certainty was that I would not get my briefcase back that weekend unless I personally went there to recover it. Mikhail would not know it was mine, and he would not know how to reach me if not at the office. Well, he would probably open the briefcase to try to find out whom it belonged to, and at that point...he'd see my law firm badge, my mail with my home address on, and...*Jeux d'Eau*. Hard to say what bothered me the most: that he saw my notes on some files I was working on, or that he saw my *Jeux d'Eau* sheet music. Should I just go get it?

I made coffee, chose a Ravel LP and put it on the turntable. I closed my eyes and imagined to be dancing on that music with Ravel. But now Ravel looked like Mikhail. I turned off the music, put on my jogging suit, and went for a run. Adam was right. I was too tired.

When I returned, I took a shower and tried to find ideas

for my weekend, but I was uninspired. I had spent the last weekends at the law firm, and I didn't have errands to run. I didn't know the city that well to find it attractive, and not enough to even be curious about it. I pulled a book and started reading, but I was distracted. I seemed to be reading music in it. I wanted to play. The piano was looking at me.

Maybe our duty is to turn painful memories into good ones.

I sat at the piano and tried to play a scale, then another one. Then I pressed the keys in random order, and I heard something I liked. Should I try to write that down? I didn't have any music paper, so I left to buy it and write, create something.

I had so many ideas. They were not organized, but they were beating in my head, and they all somehow related to that chat on Mikhail's terrace, the smell of jasmine, the flowers, the invisible water fountains that seemed to wrap our conversations, the beauty and lightness that I saw and that I felt. I wanted to write something that captured and reproduced that.

I didn't know where I could find music paper, but instead of searching the internet, I remembered seeing a little stationary store tackled between a sushi place and an ice cream parlor. I probably even stopped there once to buy something, but my memories were all fogged by the intensity of my work-schedule. In fact, I wasn't even sure there was any such place there. But I was so excited about the music that I wanted to write that I left the apartment in a rush, without double-checking if my memory of that store was correct. I was just not used not to work during the weekend. I was experiencing something new, and that made me excited, but confused too.

I walked a bit and, when I arrived in front of a used bookstore, I remembered that I had to turn right and at some point, on my left, I would find the place I was looking for. I didn't remember the names of the streets, I never noticed or paid attention to them, but I remembered the stores' signs, especially if they were colorful or somehow peculiar. So when I arrived in front of a toy store whose sign had a curious smiling cat on, I remembered it, and thought I should be close. I looked pass two doors and there it was, the door to what seemed a garage or something. I remembered there would be stairs, I had to climb two steep and old flights of stairs and then open another old, green consumed door. My place would be there. I thought.

When I arrived, and old gentleman was there rummaging through some old articles. He was tall and looked like a Santa Klaus with no beard and somewhat dirty clothes. A construction man Santa. How funny, I thought. He said "hi," as if he had seen me before, but I doubted that. He was probably just friendly to everyone, or just friendly to his customers, actual or potential, and I fit at least in one of those categories.

"Do you sell music paper?"

"You mean, *collectible* music paper, right?"

"Collectible?"

"Yes, this is not a regular stationary store. That paper here would cost you a bit more than the paper you'd buy at a regular store."

"Well, I came here to buy music paper to use it myself. I don't see the point in buying some that has been used already."

"I actually didn't think like that when I bought used music paper. I thought someone might come here, understand what's in there, and use it."

"Use it?"

"Yes. Either sell it as paper that had been used by some

famous composer, or use it to build on, develop that music. In case it hadn't been published..."

"You mean *stealing* someone else's work...?"

"It'd be one way to look at it. The other would be to make that work grow, develop, live. Give it a voice, avoid leaving it like a dead, silent paper."

"That's a nice way to look at it," I said, and actually then believed it.

I could not remember ever being there. If it really was a collectibles store, though, I would not exclude being there to buy a pen or notebook, paying what I might have thought was an outrageous amount of money, thinking one more time that Los Angeles was an insanely expensive city, and leaving completely oblivious to what I had just bought. It was indeed possible. Hard to exclude it.

"Ok, you convinced me."

"Wonderful! Want to see what I got?"

"Please."

The older gentleman moved to the back of the store where he had objects of all sorts piled up: old typewriters, photos with the most interesting and diverse frames, books, toys, carillons. Everything was placed without a logic, or if there was one, I could not see it. And everything looked dirty and neglected. I bet, if I ever was there before, I must have thought that that was a store selling used, second-hand goods, which the owner called "collectibles."

When the man reached a pile of what seemed to be old newspapers and articles, he stopped, placed his hand right in the middle of one of those piles, and pulled, with incredible precision, a few plastic bags, which I then realized contained some music papers.

"You really know where to find your things," I said.

"Yes, I have good memory, but not great organization

skills. And mostly, I'm not interested in boring orders. Order makes me sad. Mess is more creative, don't you think?"

I didn't respond, but thought that I used to think exactly like that. Now I could not afford being messy. Too risky in my job. I had to change, and I did change a lot to be a good law student, first, then a lawyer.

"Let's go to the counter. We'll have more space there, and you could look at each sheet music and decide if you are interested in getting any of them."

I nodded and followed him back to the counter.

"This sounds like it could be from the twenties," he said, pulling some yellowish paper, with some music notes and words on top of them.

"It's a song. Let me see it."

I tried to sing it in my head, but couldn't. I must have lost some of my old skills, I thought, but then realized that song wasn't written for piano. It was probably something for trumpet, or clarinet…I could not say.

"Is there a name, an autograph on it?" I asked.

"Just a scribble. Hard to decipher. But I bet it must be from someone famous," he said.

I laughed.

"And how did you conclude so?"

"We're in L.A., people sooner or later make their dreams come true."

"I wish that applied to me too," I laughed.

"Maybe you are in the right place," he said, and winked at me.

"Let's see something else," I asked, and he started staging several music paper and notes in front of me. One of them captured my interest. I could not read the music, too much of a sketch for me to make a full melody and accompaniment out of it, but the title was so enticing."

"Ocean," it was called. I tried to look closer, and it seemed that there was an article before that word, but it was too old and consumed to decipher. It could have been a "The," or an "L'," which would make my piece a French one.

"Do you think it's an 'l' or a 'the'?" I asked him.

"What do you want it to be?"

"An 'l,' would be great," I replied, although I found that question a little childish, almost like my answer, which, however, was honest. In fact, both the question and answer were.

"Why should it be an 'l' rather than a "the"?

"I guess it might make the piece, I mean, its author, French, and I could dream that it was written by one of my favorite composers."

"Ravel?"

"How do you know?"

"I wish I could tell you I can read people's mind. It's just that I know the *Bolero* and I know he composed it. And it's probably the only one that came to mind. I must confess, I don't know much about music, but...who doesn't know Ravel and his *Bolero*?"

"Yes, of course."

The sheet music was four page long, and at the bottom of the very last page there was what appeared to be a signature, impossible to read. And then, below that, what seemed to read: Mont...(real?) 2, II, 79 (or 29). Truly hard to read.

"Does the signature, place, or date tell you anything helpful?" he asked.

"Not much," I replied, "but it's enough to make me dream about the impossible. I'll buy this one."

"Don't you want to know how much it costs?"

"You'll give me a nice price," I said, and I predicted well, as the price was nice indeed, certainly not comparable to what you'd pay for a "collectible." I thanked him, and when he shook my hand to say goodbye, he told me his name was Franz. He was German. I'd have never guessed.

On the way home, I felt happy as I had not felt in a long time, and I swung my purchase as if I was swinging something that would make my weekend memorable. This is what I believed. I was also surprised to have discovered that little piece of Los Angeles. I had not gone out since I had come to L.A., not for pleasure I mean, so this experience, me, my interaction with Franz, my voice pitch, all was so new, so different.

When I arrived home, I checked the phone to see if anyone had called, but of course none had. I looked at my purchase and realized I had not bought the paper I had left to buy, and I needed it if I wanted to write. So I left again, and again without checking first where I should try to find it.

I walked for a while, and from the window of a restaurant I noticed Mikhail sitting there with a woman. They seemed to be intimate, but then they seemed to be arguing. I turned quickly hoping he had not seen me, but he had. I started walking faster, but soon enough I heard my name.

"Clara!"

I turned and saw him. He waved at me and asked me to stop. We walked toward each other and finally met, in front of a woman who was singing loudly and selling flowers. His face was sweet and he looked tired.

"I'm sorry if I stopped you. I had to talk to you."

"Sure," I said, when I noticed he was catching his breath and looked sad, or maybe it was just the loud and out-of-tune woman's song that made him or our exchange feel so.

"I'm sorry for yesterday," he said, "I was very inappropriate. I hope you can forgive me."

My mind went back to that moment we had on the balcony. Why was he apologizing?

"I...no, of course, there is no need," I rushed to say. He screened my eyes for a while, and then added,

"I hope we'll have more chances to work together in the future, and maybe you could come back for dinner sometimes, when we're back."

"Are you leaving?"

"Yes. Marina and I are leaving."

"Oh," I said, and suddenly felt sad.

"Are you going back to Moscow?"

"Not immediately. Marina is a singer. She has a tour in Europe, so I'll try to follow her in between works."

I wanted to ask who Marina was, but I didn't.

"I think I left my briefcase at your place yesterday night."

"Oh, I'm sorry about that. I'd have returned it had I noticed. My staff must have set it aside for you, but everyone left so late yesterday, and we've been busy packing. If you leave me an address and phone number, I could have it delivered to you today."

I remained silent, still digesting the news that he was leaving.

"Or I could of course send everything to the office."

"I could come pick it up, I don't want to trouble you."

"It won't be any trouble," he said, and pulled his Blackberry from his pocket to write what I would dictate.

I gave him my address and phone number, but before leaving I said,

"Thank you for what you told me yesterday. It helped. It was nice."

"It was," he said, shook my hand, and added, "good luck!"

I walked back to my place, placed my bag with the music

sheet on my desk, and did not play it. And I had not even bought the paper I needed for writing, but I no longer felt like it. I ordered pizza, and watched a movie until it was dark, then went to bed.

When I woke up the next day, it was still dark. I must have fallen asleep when it was too early. I turned the TV on to a news channel, and started sipping my coffee without paying attention. Then, when the sun came up, I checked the door to see if my newspaper had arrived, and found a box with my address handwritten on it, and a white rose wrapped around a ribbon that was keeping the box together.

I took the box inside the apartment, opened it, and there was my briefcase and a letter.

Dear Clara,

As I'm preparing to leave, I thought I should write to you to explain what I didn't have a chance to.

You were so nice yesterday when I asked you to forgive me, almost pretended I had not done anything inappropriate with you, but I did. I'm not usually that imprudent or impulsive, especially with such a beautiful, graceful, young woman like you. I should have been respectful of our professional relationship and cherish the beginning of a friendship that I hope you'll still be so kind enough to allow me to have with you.

The reason for my unforgivable behavior is that you remind me so much of a woman who broke my heart right after I bought the house for my brother. She was younger than me, like you, a pianist like you, as I gather, and we said we'd go to Paris together and spend some time there. She also loved Ravel and his music, and I came to know her because she studied with my brother. When I discovered that she had been with him while we were together, my heart broke, and I did not go to Paris as I had intended to.

I thought I should share this with you as I have been inconsiderate with you and because I pushed you to share with me your intimate story while I had not shared mine in the first place. I was also happy when you said that you had a nice time with me, on our terrace, and for even thanking me for helping you in some way. I thought about it and concluded that this might have something to deal with my intention to make good memories of the bad ones.

If that truly made you happy, Clara, I should then honor my statement and apply it to myself. I should follow Marina to Paris this time, and perhaps go see La Bélvèdere and check whether my humble reproduction of Ravel's garden is a decent one.

I hope you'll take good care of yourself and look forward to meeting you sometimes not too far in the future, promising that I'd have finally grown up by then.

Some time ago, I found this recording of Jeaux d'eau. It is claimed to be Ravel's, but who knows... In any event, I find it sublime. By now, I almost remember it by heart, so I think it's time to let it go, and that you should have it.

Hoping to give you something that will make you happy, I send you my warmest wishes of good luck, and remain sincerely and respectfully yours.

Mikhail

I placed the record on the turntable and let it play. The recording was quite remarkable, Mikhail was right, and even if it wasn't Ravel's, as with the "collectible" music sheet, it was also nice to believe that it might be the case.

When the music was over, I pulled the LP off the turntable, folded Mikhail's letter, and placed them together with my *Jeaux d'eau* and the "collectible" *Ocean* scores in the same suitcase where I had placed my letter to Ravel. I didn't feel like playing, and wanted to push the past few days in the back of my mind. Yes, I wanted to turn the bad memories into good ones. I just wasn't ready for it.

The last few days had been surreal and intense, and now I felt sad and alone. I went to my window and thought about William. Then I looked for my Blackberry, hoping to find something in there that would make me feel better, and work came to my rescue. Elizabeth had sent me an email with questions on an issue we needed to clarify before a meeting we'd have with a client the next day. That was perfect. I needed to leave my surreal and intense memories for a while, get distracted.

A few hours later, I was back to the law firm. The office was deserted, dark, and extremely cold. The air conditioning and the tinted glass had created the perfect parallel world to L.A., a very effective fridge for my heart and question marks, so that I could stop them from beating and just focus on work. I worked all day in the dim light of my lamp, while the sun was shining outside, and Mikhail had taken off to Europe.

THE END

THE STORY CONTINUES HERE

LOOKING FOR CLARA: A NOVEL

Her life has become a single, low note. Will an Italian escape strike a joyful chord in her soul?

Clara Smith seems out of tune, drifting through one empty day after another. Alone in LA for Christmas and uncertain about her new boyfriend, the pianist-turned-lawyer feels as fake as the snow. But when her firm dispatches her to Siena, Italy to lead a major project, the rhythm of the daily grind gloriously changes tempo.

Bonding with her charismatic eighty-year-old neighbor over his large collection of photographs, she uncovers a picture of a mysterious woman. And a breathtaking cross-country adventure, in search of the framed beauty who shares her name gives voice to Clara's long-silenced passions.

Can a melodious tour through vineyards and sun-drenched landscapes restore her sense of harmony?

Looking for Clara is a heartfelt journey into women's fiction. If you like deeply drawn characters, vivid settings, and romantic secrets, then you'll love Simona Grossi's life-affirming novel.

THANK YOU FOR READING THIS

Dear Reader,

Thank you for reading Like Still Water. This short story narrates events taking place in Clara's life before my first book, Looking for Clara. Clara's life after Like Still Water will change significantly, and more is coming after that. Stay tuned!

If you have enjoyed Like Still Water, please consider purchasing a copy of Looking for Clara from your favorite bookstore.

simona

ABOUT THE AUTHOR

Simona Grossi was born and raised in a small town in Italy, surrounded by books and music. She studied piano at the Conservatory and then attended law school and joined a prestigious law firm in Italy. After litigating for several years, she moved to the U.S. and joined academia. In addition to her addictions to her husband and to writing, she is also addicted to music. She graduated in classical piano from a Conservatory in Italy and is currently studying orchestra conducting. She also loves cooking, traveling, and spending time with her friends. Simona has published two novels: Looking for Clara and Frozen Butterflies. Both have received stellar reviews on Amazon and Goodreads.

facebook.com/simonawritesbooks

instagram.com/simonagrossila

amazon.com/Simona-Grossi/e/B0031D32MG

bookbub.com/authors/simona-grossi

FROZEN BUTTERFLIES: A NOVEL

The night is her closest companion. But some truths can only be found in the harsh light of day...

Susan is tormented by her hidden history. Driven by dark thoughts and sleepless nights, she forges a bond with a blogger who has troubles of his own. But when they discover a compelling, mysterious journal, sharing the excerpts with the world unleashes a dangerous attraction...

Following the writer's complex trail of clues, Susan and her accomplice unearth secrets about the enigmatic author and themselves. But when her own demons resurface, her relentless quest could push her to the edge of sanity.

Will Susan's revelations unlock a brighter future or simply magnify the darkness of the past?

Frozen Butterflies is a surreal work of literary fiction. If you like provocative prose, troubled characters, and heart-wrenching twists, then you'll love Simona Grossi's suspenseful novel.

www.ingramcontent.com/pod-product-compliance
Lightning Source LLC
Chambersburg PA
CBHW020605130626
46552CB00007B/3054